The Eggsters' Story

(Why the Chicken Crossed the Road)

By Ken Harvey

Illustrations by MarySue Hermes

Design by schererMedia
Printed in China

Harvey, Ken.
    The eggster's story : (why the chicken crossed the
road) / Ken Harvey ; illustrations by MarySue Hermes. –
1st ed.
    p. cm. – (Life in the 'fridge)
    SUMMARY: Orange Pop tells Billy, a pint-sized juice
drink, about how the Eggheads came to live in the
magical 'fridge. Then, when the mischievous Odor Boys
plant seeds of discontent in the refrigerator, it takes
the prodigal eggster to return things to egg-cellent.
    Audience: Ages 3-5.
    LCCN 2002104304
    ISBN 1-930093-17-9

    1. Homelessness—Juvenile fiction. 2. Food—Juvenile
fiction. 3. Loyalty—Juvenile fiction. [1. Homelessness
—Fiction. 2. Food—Fiction. 3. Loyalty—Fiction.]
I. Hermes, MarySue. II. Title.

PZ7.H267575Eg 2002   [E]
                              QBI02-701662

To my parents, who always
kept faith in their prodigal son. Love you.
—KH

To Jerry, my husband and best friend.
—MSH

Once in a magical land there was a magical house. Inside that house, in a corner of the kitchen, stood a magical refrigerator, and inside that refrigerator all the food came to life! There were new adventures inside the 'fridge every day.

It was a rainy day. It was damp and gloomy, even inside the 'fridge, so Billy the Kid, the half-pint juice drink, decided to visit the Icicle Pops. He loved listening to their stories about the good old days.

"Please tell me a story," begged Billy.

"Hmmmm," said Green Pop. "I think you've heard all my stories."

"Mine too," said Red Pop.

Orange Pop thought for a moment and asked, "Have I ever told you the story about how the Eggheads came to live in the 'fridge back when they were just baby Eggsters?"

Billy the Kid's eyes grew wide. "No," he said. "Please tell me!"

"Very well," answered Orange Pop. And this is the story he told . . . .

Once there was a magical farm owned by a couple named Mr. and Mrs. Spatula. On this farm lived a flock of very special chickens who laid golden eggs. Their eggs made the farmer and his wife rich. All the chickens on the farm laid golden eggs except for one chicken. Her name was Janice.

Janice was special too, but nobody knew this except Mr. Spatula. Janice loved adding numbers. She walked around the farm counting seeds, or plants, or trees, or anything else she could find to practice her special talent. But the other chickens ignored Janice because she didn't lay any eggs at all.

Even Mrs. Spatula disliked Janice. "She's a useless chicken," she complained. "We should get rid of her!"

But Mr. Spatula loved Janice and protected her, even though she didn't lay golden eggs for him. He had a kind heart, and Janice always helped him when he needed to count his golden eggs.

One night while Mr. and Mrs. Spatula were asleep, all the chickens were stolen—except for Janice. The farmer and his wife didn't know what to do. They searched high and low, but they could not find the chickens.

After a year without their chickens and no more golden eggs, Mr. and Mrs. Spatula ran out of money. They were hungry. Without money, they could not buy food.

Janice tried to cheer Mr. Spatula up, but all she could do was count. What he really needed was more golden eggs.

Mrs. Spatula always complained she was hungry. She told Mr. Spatula that Janice's time was up. Unless she began laying eggs, Janice was going into the soup pot!

Well, that very afternoon, out of the blue, Janice began clucking wildly. She sat on her nest and laid six eggs! When Mr. and Mrs. Spatula heard all the noise, they ran into the henhouse to see what was happening. But when they looked into the nest, instead of finding six golden eggs, they saw six ordinary eggs.

Mrs. Spatula was very angry. She said it was time to make chicken noodle soup. She stomped into the house to get the soup pot ready. Mr. Spatula told Janice to take her six eggs and run. He told her about a magical house far, far away where her little Eggsters could live. And that's just where she headed!

Janice walked and walked with her Eggsters tucked under her wing, trying to keep them safe and warm. Every time they stopped to rest for the night, instead of telling them bedtime stories, she counted.

One day Janice stopped walking and stared across the street at a lovely little house. It said "Cold Sweet Home" on the mailbox.

"Kids," she said, "this is the magical house Mr. Spatula told me about on the day we left the farm. It will be our new home. I'm sure we'll be safe here." The Eggsters were very excited!

Janice crossed the road with her children. [Now you know why the chicken crossed the road!] She walked up the driveway and set the eggsters down on the front stoop.

Just then the door opened. A man with a kind voice looked at Janice and smiled. "You must be tired after your long trip. Wouldn't you like to rest in the henhouse out back? I'll take care of your little ones."

Janice clucked gratefully and headed out back.

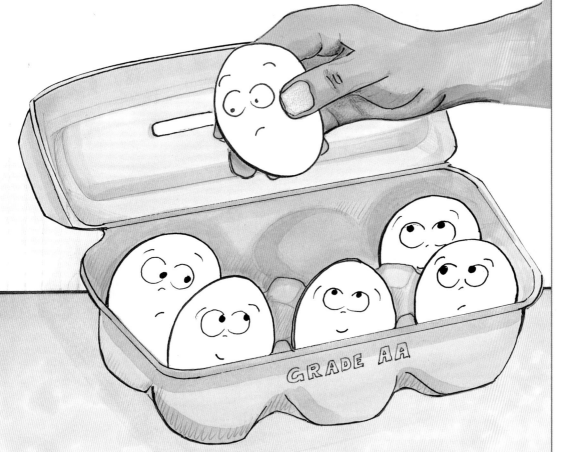

Two big hands reached down, picked up the Eggsters and carried them into the house. In the kitchen, the man put the Eggsters in a carton, opened the refrigerator door and gently set them on a shelf.

Without their mother, the Eggsters were a little scared. What would they do now?

"We should find another place to live," said Hard-Boiled. He was their leader.

"How do we do that?" cried the Soft-Boiled twins.

"I don't care what we do," said Over Easy. "Let's just do something."

"No," Sunny said. "We should stay because Mother said we'll be safe here."

Then Benedict Arnold Eggster spoke up. Everyone just called him Ben. "We're not going to make it. I'm out of here!" With that, he jumped out of the 'fridge, cracking his little head as he hit the floor.

The next thing he knew, he was back outside on the doormat. "Who needs them anyway?" Ben said.

"I'll be fine on my own, and I'll find a better place to live!" Then he rolled away without looking back.

In all the excitement, at first the Eggsters didn't see Ben leave. They were busy meeting their new neighbors. They met two gallons of milk named Frank and Sally, Armando the Policeman who was the refrigerator freshener, Gus the sports drink, the Cool Cubes and the Icicle Pops. Even the mischief-making Odor Boys stopped by to say hello. But after meeting the Eggsters, the Odor Boys huddled in a corner and whispered to one another.

"Why are there only five of them?" asked one of the Odor Boys. "It looks like their carton was made for six."

"Yeah, you're right," said another. "I'll bet they ATE him!" he exclaimed.

"Yuck! That's sick!" they all shouted. Then they returned to the group, whispering among themselves.

But the Eggsters were having the time of their lives. They began adding up numbers for their new friends. Everyone was very impressed—everyone except the Odor Boys.

"What's 2+2?" asked Frank.

"That's easy . . . 4," said Over Easy.

"Then what's 5+5?" asked Gus.

"It's 10!" the Eggsters yelled together.

"Here's one!" yelled one of the Odor Boys. "What's one million, three hundred and forty-eight thousand times four hundred million?"

Everyone turned and looked at the Odor Boys.

$$\begin{array}{r} 2 \\ +2 \\ \hline 4 \end{array}$$

$$5 + 5 = 10$$

"That's too hard," said Gus.

The Odor Boys laughed. "Okay," said one. "This is easy. What's six Eggsters minus one?"

Suddenly the Eggsters began to cry.

"What's wrong?" asked Orange Pop.

"Our brother Ben ran away!" the Eggsters cried.

"They ATE him!" shouted the Odor Boys.

Everyone was shocked. "What are you talking about?" Armando asked.

"Where else could he be?" asked the Odor Boys.

The Eggsters cried harder. "We did NOT eat our brother!" shouted Sunny. "We miss him."

"I don't miss him," said Hard-Boiled. "He left us here alone. We don't need him anymore." The other Eggsters stared at their brother and fell silent, but the Odor Boys were laughing to themselves at all the trouble they had caused.

Just then the refrigerator door opened and a cracked, very dirty and tired Benedict Arnold Eggster was placed beside his brothers and sisters.

"Ben!" shouted Sunny. "Are you okay?"

"Welcome home," said the Soft-Boiled twins.

"Hey, Brother, how's it going?" Over Easy asked.

Only Hard-Boiled remained silent.

"Doesn't anyone care about where I've been?" Ben asked.

Green Pop spoke up. "Your brothers and sisters love you. They are happy you have returned. That's more important than why you left or where you've been."

As they all helped clean Ben's shell, he told them about his adventure. Ben had missed his mother so much he decided to go out back behind the magical house to find her. In the driveway a crow tried to peck open his shell. Then a dog drooled on him. A nearsighted squirrel thought he was a gigantic acorn and tried to bury him. Finally, he rolled into a mud puddle before the kind man from the house brought him back inside.

"I'm sorry I was so angry," said Hard-Boiled, nuzzling his brother.

"And I'm sorry that I left you all behind," Ben replied.

"Look! He's cracking up!" said one of the Odor Boys, because their fun was being spoiled.

"Yeah," said another, "and now his brains are scrambled!"

But nothing could stop the happy celebration. Once again, everything was "egg-cellent" inside the magical 'fridge.

Orange Pop finished his story and smiled at Billy. "Did you enjoy that story?" he asked.

"Oh, yes!" Billy exclaimed. "I've always wondered how Ben cracked his shell, but I was afraid I might hurt his feelings if I asked."

"Ben is very proud of that crack in his shell. It's a very important reminder for all of us," said Orange Pop. "Do you know why?"

"No," said Billy.

All the Icicle Pops gathered around Billy and hugged him. "It reminds us to stay together and to take care of one another," said Orange Pop.

"Just like the Eggsters!" laughed Billy.

By wisdom a house is built,
And through understanding it is established;
Through knowledge its rooms are filled
With rare and beautiful treasures.

Proverbs 24:3-4